Mary A. De Vere

Love Songs

and other poems

Mary A. De Vere

Love Songs
and other poems

ISBN/EAN: 9783337265335

Printed in Europe, USA, Canada, Australia, Japan

Cover: Foto ©Andreas Hilbeck / pixelio.de

More available books at **www.hansebooks.com**

LOVE SONGS,

AND

OTHER POEMS.

BY

MARY AINGE DE VERE.

I do but sing because I must,
And pipe but as the linnets sing.
TENNYSON.

NEW YORK:
FIFTH AVENUE PUBLISHING COMPANY.
1870.

TO

ROBERT ROOSEVELT,

THE KIND AND SYMPATHETIC COUNSELLOR OF IMPATIENT YOUTH,

ACROSS A GULF OF FORTY YEARS

THIS SLENDER THREAD IS THROWN,

NOT WITHOUT HOPE OF

A MORE SUBSTANTIAL BRIDGE TO FOLLOW;

A BRIDGE THAT

MAY SUSTAIN EVEN THE UNITED WEIGHT OF

CRITIC

AND

AUTHOR.

CONTENTS.

LOVE SONGS.

FIRST POEMS.

LOVE SONGS.

THE DEPARTURE.

SHE threw him a rose as he turned away,
    He passed it lightly from hand to lip,
Then, with a smile more grave than gay,
    Touched his cap with a finger-tip;
Went away, with his martial tread,
To swell the lists of the early dead.

She watched him passing over the lawn,
    Down through the roses, out of the gate;
Have the light and life of the morning gone,
    Or is her young heart left desolate?
She threw him a rose, and her eyelids fell—
Did she throw him her own proud heart as well?

He did not question, he never dreamed;
    He was too honest by far to guess

That her act was aught but the thing it seemed,
　Coquettish, pretty, and meaningless;
But he thought of her eyes as she said good-by,
Calm and bright as the morning sky.

The sun struck gold from her rippled hair,
　Her light scarf trailed in the morning dew,
Her arms hung listless, and white, and bare,
　As slowly she paced the garden through;
Never a sob, though her heart was torn,
But she smiled at herself with a strange self-scorn.

" Too late, too late!" was the moan she made,
　Only that and her long-drawn sighs;
" She does not love me!" was all he said,
　As the great tears dropped from his downcast eyes,
And he folded close to his faithful breast
The rose whose blushing was love confessed.

So his soldierly step he bent
　Down to the village to meet the train,
And out from his peaceful home he went,
　Never in life to return again;
But early in autumn a coffin came,
The rough lid stamped with his age and name.

Lonely he sleeps mid sun and shower,
   Where marbles glimmer and willows wave;
But a woman's heart, and a faded flower,
   Lie buried deep in the soldier's grave.
Does he know it? Ah, who can tell
If at last he is sure that she loved him well!

LOVE'S LONGING.

ONLY to see your face—
   To look on it once again;
Whatever the time or place,
   Or whether in joy or pain:
A look of a moment long,
   A glimpse as you passed me by—
Ah, love! the prayer of the heart is strong,
   However subdued its cry.

Only to hear your voice,
   Angry, or proud, or meek—
Belovèd, I have no choice—
   Only to hear you speak.
A word from your lips to hear,
   Whatever its tone might be ;
I would not care if you cursed me, dear,
   So that you spoke to me!

Only to touch you, sweet,
　Passing by in a crowd—
You would hear my wild heart beat,
　Telling its bliss aloud:
Only to see your face,
　To know that you spoke to me,
To touch your hand for a moment's space
　I would barter eternity!

ENDED.

OVER and done, and the sun has set;
   Day is hiding behind the sea;
Over and done! Shall we both forget?
  Who knows what is yet to be?
    I know what will come at the last of all—
     Deep, deep rest, under sun and moon;
    The roses are withered, the dead leaves fall,
     And snow will be falling soon.

Over and done! Oh, beautiful day!
  Did you part in anger or scorn?
Night comes sullen and cold and gray,
  But you will return at morn!
    And smile on the world with a tender light,
     Oh, me! for my endless pain!
    For a day that has passed from my longing sight,
     Never to dawn again.

EASTWARD.

I LOOK out over the fair, green land,
    And I feel the warm tears start;
The sun goes down in the glowing west,
    But eastward flies my heart.
        Oh, but to be a happy bird,
            To fly from this valley-nest,
        Over the purple mountain-tops,
            Away to my true-love's breast.

There in the East a city lies,
    Splendid with dome and spire;
There in the East are the dreamy eyes,
    And the lips of my long desire.
        Oh, if I were a happy bird
            Flying out of the West,
        Would he open his window wide,
            And give me another nest?

OAKLAND, CAL., *June* 7, 1863.

DO YOU REMEMBER?

Do you remember, darling?
    The mist from the meadow crept
Over the level landscape,
    Moonlight and silence slept.

Do you remember, darling?
    We stood in the open door,
And our shadows fell together,
    Blent on the moonlit floor.

Do you remember, darling?
    You gave me a soft brown braid,
And a rose-bud out of your bosom,
    To bear on my heart, you said.

Do you remember, darling?
    I'm wearing your keepsakes yet,
But you seem to have quite forgotten;
    Why cannot I, too, forget?

LOVE'S VALUE.

WHAT is love worth? A smile,
  Such as a maiden to her mirror gives,
Curling her hair the while.

What is love worth? A sigh,
Breath from the fulness of a youthful heart,
Whose pleasures satisfy.

What is love worth? A tear,
The lightest ever dropped from happy eyes,
When joy and hope are near.

What is love worth? Ah, sweet,
Is love worth this true, tender heart, I lay
At your dear maiden feet?

2

AN APRIL DAY.

ALONG a winding woodland path,
　　Through leafy arches low and dim,
Toward the sweet murmur of a brook,
　　In silent mood, I followed him.

The April sky hung soft and dark,
　　Divided between smile and frown ;
By turns the large, warm rain-drops fell,
　　By turns the yellow sun looked down.

Nor bird nor bee with music broke
　　The charm of silence in the air ;
Only afar the dreamy voice
　　Of flowing water murmured there.

We loitered slowly and apart ;
　　I moved behind with bated breath ;

That hour I would have followed him
Unto the very gates of death !

And he—he held the brush aside,
He shook the boughs that crossed my way :
How should I dream his love was like
That sweet, uncertain April day ?

Beside the stream he paused and turned,
Awaiting me with hands outspread :
" Oh, come ! " he broke the silent spell,
" Here are the violets," he said—

" The sweetest, earliest of the year,
See where they glimmer few and frail."
" Oh, dearest, gather them for me ;
And when their scent and beauty fail—

" I'll keep them sacred for the sake
Of your dear eyes, so soft and blue."
He turned and clasped me in his arms,
He seemed to look me through and through.

With one long, eager. asking gaze,
Ah! well, he kissed my lips and brow.

And hid my violets in his breast—
And all is but a memory now.

.   .   .   .

From spring to spring my life goes on,
　Not quite bereft of love and grace,
Nor all o'ershadowed in the loss
　Of one beloved and vanished face.

But when the violets first unclose,
　My heart counts up her lonely years;
And when the April rain-drops fall,
　I cannot keep my foolish tears.

TO ———.

I.

LOW darts the light across the Western wold;
    Long, quivering beams lie on the silent sea;
The East is blue, the West is wrapped in gold—
    Clothed as my spirit is in love for thee.

II.

From the clear waves the sunbeams melt away;
    Above the far horizon's rim I see
One faint, white sail against the fading day—
    As cold and faint as is thy love for me.

OAKLAND, CAL., *June* 15, 1863.

ONE LITTLE LOCK.

ONE little lock of your hair,
  One little curl to press
On my lips and my longing heart—
  Darling, one little tress!

Oh, what a simple boon!
  You have not the heart to refuse—
So great a treasure for me to gain,
  So little for you to lose.

You cannot refuse me this;
  And, dear, wherever I go,
I'll always keep it hidden away—
  No one shall ever know.

When I go to my lonely rest,
  In the desolate, silent night,

I may kiss it, and sleep, and dream
   Of a day that was fair and bright,

Of a day that was sweet and brief—
   I have no wish to complain,
But it seems that I long and yearn
   For a gleam of its light again.

Belovèd, I never thought,
   Then, when my world was fair,
That ever I'd ask in vain
   For a curl of your golden hair.

One little lock of your hair,
   On my desolate heart to lie;
One little tress to keep and caress,
   For the sake of a day gone by!

CONTRADICTION.

SHE sat and looked at the falling leaves,
　　Looked at the sunless autumn sky,
And " Oh, that I were a leaf! " she said,
　" Calmly to fade and die;
　　　Drop and be covered with gentle snow,
　　　Never another spring to know."

Then, as the solemn night came down,
　She saw heaven's jewels gleam afar,
Faithful and tender and pure; she said:
　" Oh, that I were a star,
　　　Over my lover, by sea or shore,
　　　To shine forever and evermore !"

SEVERED.

TAKE my hand and say good-by,
  Love, our paths must separate lie;

Far apart our lives shall be
As those lands that shore the sea;

There must live no sign or token
Of the bond that Fate hath broken;

Nor a ship or bark be seen
On the waste that lies between;

Nor a hand held out to thee,
Whatsoe'er thy danger be;

Parted as the mountains stand,
By long leagues of valley-land;

Where no laughing waters flow,
Nor the birds fly to and fro;

Separate as the planets are,
Each a pale but living star;

Each a prisoner in his place,
Looking down with patient face;

Parted, parted, evermore,
As by sea, the shore from shore;

As by valleys mountains are,
As by spaces, star from star.

When the end of all has come,
And the lips are closed and dumb,

When the eyes that watch and weep,
Fold themselves in endless sleep,

And our souls are free of pain,
Will God let us meet again?

DECREED.

HERE, in the silent night,
When even those who love me best are gone,
Through the dark house there glimmers not a light,
    I sit alone:

    Alone as I shall be
When I am still, and breath hath passed away;
And there is nothing left to earth of me,
    But coffined clay.

    Fancy me dead—
Lying beyond the clasping of thy love,
Never again to raise my wearied head,
    Or breathe, or move:

All my heart cold,
Colder than even now, snow-cold as it may seem,
My ended life, like to a tale half told—
A broken dream.

Thou wouldst live on:
God sends not suffering to smite or slay,
But as the night's last hour—the darkest one—
Just ere the day,

To make more dear
The longed-for splendors of approaching light;
Love, thy soul's purity, by every tear
Is made more white.

Take up the cross—
And take for evermore farewell of me ;
But oh, beloved, believe, the greater loss
Is mine—in thee !

WHEN WE ARE PARTED.

WHEN we are parted—when I have seen you, darling,
  For the last time in all my lonely life—
When these strange hours are ended, and within my
    bosom
  Reigns cold despair, where now is eager strife;
When the long kiss is given, the farewell spoken,
  And that last precious hour has flitted by;
When my close clasp of your dear hand is severed,
  Will not God pity me, and bid me die?

When we are parted, dearest—when no longer
  I dare to hope or dream that we shall meet,
Would my cheek burn as now, my heart beat stronger,
  To hear the coming of your well-known feet?
Would the mere sense of duty so estrange me
  That I could pass you, darling, coldly by,

Belovèd, ere the world and time so change me,
  May God be merciful, and let me die!

When we are parted—not as now, for hours,
  Whose lengths go by in mingled joy and pain,
But always parted—will the birds and flowers
  Come back, and go and come and go again?
And ever newly, with the spring-tide waking,
  Will memory flood the soul, and dim the eye?
Ah, love, the strongest heart bears but one breaking:
  When the spring comes without thee, I shall die!

AT THE FERRY.

NOT a kiss—not a tear—
　　Not even so much
As an uttered word,
　—Not a touch!

Oh, the passion, the pain,
　So coldly to part!
But I gave you one look,
　—And my heart.

You will pardon me then,
　And you understand
That my soul is yours,
　—Not my hand.

WHY?

DARK hair, and dark, dark eyes,
  And a smile so strange and sweet,
That, were I bound for Paradise,
  Thy smile could stay my feet :
    Though my heart break for love of thee,
    Belovèd, never smile on me !

I come—as pilgrims come—
  To worship at a shrine ;
Be thou as marble, cold and dumb,
  To each wild prayer of mine :
    Though I should die, beseeching thee,
    Belovèd, never answer me !

AN HOUR.

WAS it an hour? It seemed to me
     A lifetime while we sat alone,
The room as silent as a tomb might be,
   But for one tone—

Like the sound ripples make,
   Breaking forever on the strand;
Thy voice the eager waves, my heart
   The dumb, cold sand.

Did I not hear the words
   Such as all lovers speak?
Did I not feel thy breath
   Warm on my cheek?

Were not my features cold
   As those of death?

3

Did not my lips deny
  One answering breath ?

I could have yielded, then,
  All this world's bliss,
Just to have offered thee
  One lover's kiss—

My highest hopes on earth,
  Even those fixed above,
Just to have answered thee,
  Saying, " I love ! "

Didst thou deem me unkind,
  Thy passion, thy prayer,
Thy breathless tenderness,
  Wasted in air—

I could have laid me down,
  Low at thy feet;
I could have welcomed death,
  Calling it sweet;

I could have given away,
  In tears, my soul,
Just to have healed thy heart,
  And made it whole!

DOUBT.

IN June, when the roses hung
  Over the hedges, heavy with dew,
And softly the skylark sung
  Out of his cloud in the endless blue,
    I walked through the summer land,
      A delicate foot kept step with mine,
    In mine there nestled a darling hand,
      And life was a thing divine!

But now, if the roses burn,
  Pouting their lips for the sun to kiss;
If all things lovely return,
  And only her beautiful face I miss,
    What shall I say to this heart of mine?
      This heart that is only waiting to break,
    Waiting, waiting the word or sign,
      To break for her darling sake!

THE ANSWER.

YES, you are kind, and tender, and brave, as a
   man should be;
And your heart, I know, is faithful—you have proven
   it so to me;
And you love me well—yet, I tell you, 'twere better
   that you should die
Than pass by all other women, to wed such a one as I !

Even, dear, if I loved you—supposing it might be so—
But that is the idlest dreaming, the vainest your soul
   can know—
Years ago—so many, I count them over with pain—
Love came, possessed, and forsook me—it never will
   come again !
Only once in a lifetime, the poet says, in his song:
" Ah, well! 'tis often enough, God knows, let life be
   ever so long !"

I pray, as I never have prayed to be saved from woe
    or crime,
That my passionate heart may be shielded from loving
    a second time!

You are wiser, more calm than I; 'tis plain and pleas-
    ant to you;
Your instincts are all unerring, your judgment so pure
    and true;
Love is your crown of glory, the seal of a bliss di-
    vine:
Love is the crown of thorns and the scourge to a
    soul like mine!

Not that I am so weak, or wicked, or fickle, as women
    go;
I would not pain you, dear, by seeming to reckon my-
    self too low:
But I know that, if I had courage to speak the whole
    of my mind,
You would no longer wonder that I call you foolish
    and blind.

I can fancy so well the change that would come o'er
    your handsome face,
If I should open my heart to you and show you that
    dreary place—
The ruined shrine where passion's fire burned out in
    the days gone by,
Where only the black, charred embers, and the cold,
    white ashes lie !

And strangest of all, it seems to me, that no outward
    · scars I bear
Of the wounds of my terrible battle, when victory
    meant despair;
I have won and worn my laurels—do you know that I
    wear them now—
Though there is not a silver thread in my hair, nor
    a wrinkle upon my brow ?

And men still find me beautiful, and come and kneel
    at my feet;
But I shudder, and turn away—away from the lov-
    ing eyes I meet !

It seems a strange and terrible thing—life's wine
    should be wasted so,
And love's one tender flower be cast on a grave that
    is heaped with snow!

So, good-by, and God bless you! Believe it a kindly
    fate
That severs us here forever—we met each other too
    late;
And I must go my way through the world alone until
    I die,
And when you are older and wiser, you'll be glad that
    I passed you by!

DENIAL.

I DO not love you—not a bit;
　And yet, how strange it seems!—your touch
Is not unpleasant—far from it;
　Why, if I loved you much and much,
I cannot fancy that your kiss
Would thrill me any more than this!

I do not love you—oh, I'm sure—
　But when you come, you're welcome still;
Your heart is all so kind and pure,
　It can but merit my good-will:
I know I'm always glad to hear
Your kindly voice, and know you near.

I do not love you in the least,
　And yet you're surely dear to me;
And, should I look from West to East,
　No face more precious can I see;
And should I hear that you were wed—
I think the news would strike me dead!　.

WAITING.

SHE dropped the curtain-fold and turned,
   And looked no more on star or cloud;
Within, the lamp and firelight burned;
   Her mother's picture, tranquil-browed,
Looked down and watched her face to face.
Unheeding, full of saddest grace,
She knelt beside her cushioned chair,
And loosed the braids of yellow hair
That shaded pensive cheek and brow;
   Then clasped her hands above her head,
And leaning, watched the drowsy fire
   Drop down its ashes white and dead.

For hope deferred had made her sick—
   Sick, sick, unto the heart's deep core;
Long hours she heard the slow clock tick,
   And listened to the sounds without;
   And now in fear and now in doubt,
   And every foot that passed the door,

Seemed treading swiftly o'er her heart.
Anon, with sudden, joyous start,
  She raised her head; quick blushes came!
She heard his foot upon the floor,
  Her parted lips had formed his name—
And then the fire burned as before;
  The clock ticked on; and, just the same,
Unmoved and calm, her mother's face
Looked down and watched her from its place.

SONNET.

DARKNESS.

LONG, long ago in June—sweet, fragrant June!
   The shining stars, like silver lamps hung high,
Burned purely, in the absence of the moon;
   Darkly the hill-tops rose against the sky;
Dark was the lane; but from one window streamed
   A long, bright ray that crossed the garden's space,
And struck the hedge where snowy hawthorn gleamed.
   I felt the dew's cool softness on my face,
As up and down we strayed, hand clasping hand—
   It was my one sweet glimpse of Paradise!
The dim-lit Heaven, the dark and dewy land,
   Thy dewy lips—thy dark and tender eyes—
Nor day can ever dawn so golden bright to me
As that still, moonless night, in the long lane with
    thee.

GOOD-BY.

ROUND the veranda-railing the red, red roses
    hung;
  Under the early sunlight the garden-walks were dry;
And light-hearted birds were singing. What was the
    song they sung?
  Sweetly they chirped and trilled it—"Good-by,
    good-by, and good-by!"

There on the steps we stood, a sad little while to-
    gether:
  Never a touch of the hand or lips, not a tear nor an
    uttered sigh;
But we played with the hanging roses—talked of the
    pleasant weather,
  Our hearts repeating forever—"Good-by, good-by,
    and good-by!"

FORSAKEN.

HOW many waves, with their caps of foam,
  Rise and fall betwixt thee and home?
How many leagues of restless sea
Separate thee, my beloved, from me?

Bound for that land, so far away,
The tall ships pass from the open bay;
But alone, alone, on the lonely land,
With desolate, breaking heart I stand—

And follow the sails with yearning gaze,
Till they glimmer down in the ocean-haze;
For so it seemeth my soul may be
A little the nearer, beloved, to thee.

ACROSTIC.

A STAR that sees its image lie,
Deep where still waves reflect the sky,
A joyous wind that wanders by;

Roses within the heart of June,
A snow-drift shining to the moon,
Noon's glory over land and sea—
So seems thy beauty unto me;
Oh, deep and sweet, and fresh and pure,
May thy soul's loveliness endure!

FOR EVERMORE.

PARTED forever, yes, forever parted!
   To meet and greet you calmly, as a friend,
And yet, beloved, to know you broken-hearted—
   Is this the bitter end?

Is this the end? Here, in my lonely chamber,
   I wake at midnight, and alone I weep,
Where I had hoped to hear you softly breathing
   In your sweet, peaceful sleep:

Where I had hoped to hear your footstep echo,
   Your ringing laugh, your voice so childish sweet,
Making me answer—where I had hoped, at even,
   Your welcome kiss to meet!

Parted forever? Ah, as widely parted
   As if the solemn ocean rolled between—

So vast the gulf that severs utterly
  What is from what has been!

Parted forever!—then, when we stood all mutely,
  And your arms held me, clinging close and fast,
Was it the last—that silent kiss you gave me—
  For evermore the last?

Sweet was the tempting cup we drank together;
  Pausing ere yet the sweetest drop was drained,
We moved apart. And my heart broke, in keeping
  Your woman's soul unstained!

You went, with steadfast eyes, and face uplifted;
  Is there a long, long pilgrimage to make?
Trust me, beloved, I will take heart and courage,
  For your most precious sake.

To live—to move—each in our separate places;
  Sometimes to smile, and talk in friendly wise,
Across that dark abyss wherein lies buried,
  Our key of Paradise!

4

The gate is shut and locked, the lovely portal
    That we had hoped to pass some future time,
Hand given to hand, heart unto heart, repeating
    Love's old sweet rhyme.

Dear, ended hope! the weary night and morning
    Follow each other through the weary year;
For me no moment of the day or darkness
    Will bring thee kind and near.

Is there a recompense for souls that suffer,
    Bearing life's heavy cross through ice and fire?
Is there in heaven, at last, the sweet fulfilment
    Of earth's long, deep desire?

Oh! if I might believe, and trusting, follow
    Thy patient footsteps to the heavenly shore;
But, love, I only know that we are parted—
    Parted for evermore!

FRAGMENT.

THE waves sweep up and down, caressing the dead
    white sand
That lies as mute as a long cold corpse under the kiss
    of love,
The passionate touches and praying to which there is
    no reply,
Nor even a hope of answer, though love's deep heart
    should break,
As the long, quick, eager billows break and fall at my
    feet!

Is there no hope of answer?   Never again on earth,
Never from swift uplifted eyes that made me once
    sweetest speech,
Never from tender lips or the blushes on cheek and
    brow?

No more words in the low, sweet voice that sank like
    dew on my soul—
No more words, not any, not even a sigh!

Do you listen, my dearest? The great dark earth is
    still ;
Into the waste of waters the moon glides down like a
    ghost,
Whom the breath of the morn surprises. . . . Still—
    it is all so still,
That it seems you cannot but hear me, tho' you were
    buried deep,
And the clods and stones fell a long way down to strike
    on your coffin-lid !

Oh, love, when I heard them falling, beating your
    tender breast,
I thought, " What horrible dream is this? It cannot
    possess me long :
Oh, that I might awaken—now, ere my strong heart
    break ! "
And then, as a dreamer will, I strove to dissolve the
    spell,

Clenched my hands together, and stamped on the solid
    ground,
Crying: "Awaken, heart!" lone heart, that can never
    awake!

And I saw, in my dreaming, the fresh, green sod
    smoothed over your quiet bed,
And I gathered a white field-daisy that clung to the
    tangled grass;
—The spade's sharp edge had cruelly severed the
    slender stem.
You were always so fond, so fond of the common
    wayside flowers!—
I carried the daisy home for your sake, when I left
    you sleeping there.

Sleeping, dear? Are you sleeping too soundly to hear
    my cry?—
Oh, dead! Are you dead, beloved, as this white sand
    under my feet?
Was it a handful of dust that I worshipped so tenderly?
The pallid face with eyelids sealed, and lips so passive
    and cold;

The coffined, enshrouded form, with patient and listless hands—
Voiceless, sightless, unheeding! Was that, indeed,
what I loved?

Dear, there is light in heaven, though the fair, white
moon is gone;
The blue above is purer, the stars grow distant and
dim;
For the gate of the day swings open, and far in the
yellow east
The long, dark woods come slowly out of the shadow
of night;
The fields grow golden and white with their treasures
of waving grain,
And the world into light awakens—the dark, dark
hour—it is past!

. . . .

SUSPENSE.

AH! the sun was less than golden,
  And the world was less than fair;
Silver sheen of tender moonlight,
  Crimson cloud in morning air;
Gorgeous hues of glowing summer,
  When a million blossoms shook—
Cold and sombre—while I waited
    For a look!

Ah, the wind had lost its music,
  And the sea I loved was dumb;
Birds forgot their merry trilling,
  And the bees their busy hum;
There was naught of tune or sweetness
  In the thousand sounds I heard:
All was discord, while I waited
    For a word!

Ah, my soul forgot her journey,
    Flush of hope and throb of pain,
Wine of earth and draught celestial,
    Honor's crown and labor's gain!
Death and life were idle shadows,
    Even heaven's immortal bliss
Paled and faded, while I waited
    For a kiss!

ONCE.

A RED September sunset stained the sky,
  Through the wide-open windows, high and bare,
  Came sudden balmy wafts of fragrant air;
Alone we sat together, you and I,
  Five years ago my friend, this very day;
But ere the sunset faded you were gone,
  And one by one the faint beams crept away,
And I sat looking at the stars alone.
  Youth lay around me, and the autumn sky
Sparkled with stars, like points of living light;
  My heart seemed boundless as heaven's arches high,
For every star of hope shone keen and bright;
  And stars and hopes were myriad—bitter tears
  Since have outnumbered both, through five long
    weary years.

LOVE.

MY heart o'erflows as a cup with wine;
    Drink, belovèd, the draught is thine;
Drown thy passion, thine eager pain—
Then give me the empty cup again.

Drink, belovèd, and drench thy soul;
But keep me the goblet pure and whole;
Give it unbroken back, I pray—
It may fill to o'erflowing another day.

FIRST POEMS.

A MOTHER'S OFFERING.

1 8 6 1.

GO, at thy country's call.
Whatever gentle bonds may hold thee here,
Whatever tender claims may seem more dear,
Thy duty!—first of all.

Go! And God guard thy way—
Through all the hidden dangers of the night,
Through pain and peril—to the dawning light
Of peaceful day.

Go! Thy young heart is brave.
Battle for right with all thy strength and will.
Shouldst thou not triumph, thou at least canst fill
A soldier's grave.

Go! If the cause be won,
On the bright record free of stain or blot
Thy name shall shine forever; but if not,
God's will be done!

Go! I can say adieu
As gladly as a greeting home to thee,
And look my last through smiles, if thou wilt be
Firm, brave, and true.

Go! my one child! my joy—
Unto his country for whatever fate,
By these last tears, O Heaven! I consecrate
My only boy!

IN SPRING.

OH, the heartache and the pain,
    When the snow-drifts fall away,
And the violet faces rise,
    From the clay!

I had rather far be dead,
    When I hear the robins sing,
As they build their leafy nests
    In the spring.

Once I blossomed sweet and fair,
    Once I sang the livelong day,
Once my happy nest I made,
    In the May.

But my song and beauty failed,
    And my little ones took wing,
And my heart's an empty nest,
    Now, in spring.

FLIGHT.

O SWIFT and happy things!
    O birds, that cleave the blue, bright air!
I envy you those strong and rapid wings,
    Your freedom everywhere.

I weary of the ground;
    I long to rise and soar away
Into that silence where there breaks no sound—
    The brighter, better day.

I need such joyous strength!
    —Dear soul, you wear an earthly chain;
Your freedom, late it may be, comes at length,
    Nor ever ends again.

The birds, so fair and free,
    They fall and die upon the sod;
But those strong wings wherewith death gifteth thee,
    Will fly as far as God!

MY BOAT.

INTO the twilight, into the night,
My little boat sailed away;
Past the lingering sunset light,
At the gates of day;
Past the headlands, lofty and dim,
And the light-house spark,
Over the misty ocean-rim,
Dropped into the dark.

The soft waves rolled to my waiting feet,
And went and came;
I saw the sea and the moonrise meet,
In a silver flame;
Saw the white clouds drift and float
On the endless blue,
And daylight break—but my little boat,
It was lost to view.

5

The waves sing on, with a strange delight,
    Round the pleasant coast,
And sometimes a pure sail moves in sight,
    Like a gliding ghost;
But mine, that went o'er a sunset sea,
    From the safe, green shore,
I know it has faded away from me,
    To return no more!

FAITH TREMBLING.

WERE I a happy bird
    Building my little nest each early spring,
It might be easy then to keep God's word,
    His praise to sing;
Easy to live content,
    Tending my little ones—of love secure,
Knowing no agony for time misspent,
    Or thought impure!

Were I a butterfly,
    A bright winged creature of the sunshine born,
Idle and lovely I could live and die
    Without self-scorn;
I need not fear
    To take my utmost will of summer sweet—
Nor dread when the swift end came near,
    My Judge to meet!

If I were only made
   Patient, and calm, and pure, as angels are,
I had not been so doubtful—sore afraid
   Of sin and care;
It would seem sweet and good
   To bear the heavy cross that martyrs take,
The passion and the pain of womanhood
   For my Lord's sake.

But strong, and fair, and young,
   I dread my glowing limbs—my heart of fire,
My soul that trembles like a harp full strung
   To keen desire!
Oh, wild and idle words!
   Will God's large charity and patience be
Given unto butterflies and singing birds,
   And not to me?

ROSE AND LILY.

PUT a rose beside her head,
   She was fair as roses are—
Fair and sweet—but she is dead;
   Move with care.
Warm hands, touch her soft and light;
   Will she know how light and kind,
Lying, robbed of sound and sight,
   Deaf and blind!

Put a lily in her breast,
   Do not fear to shame it so;
She was fairest, purest, best—
   Whisper low.
Softly speak, dear friend, and move;
   Though this be but senseless clay,
Is the soul we know and love
   Far away?

MORNING LAND.

DEEP in the dreamy distance,
   Traced on a faint-blue sky,
Lonely and fair and solemn,
   The hills of morning lie.

A pilgrim, I wander onward,
   Far from that morning land;
The pathway is rough and stony,
   Through regions of barren sand.

And my feet they are slow and weary,
   But often I turn and gaze
Back at that peaceful landscape,
   Veiled in its golden haze.

There is but the gentle outline
   Of valley and mountain-land,
But memory touches the picture
   With tender and faithful hand.

Out of the far-off dimness
  The places I loved appear,
Orchard and field and meadow,
  The house with the willows near;

The porch where the woodbine-blossoms
  Their cups of perfume swung,
And quaint old rooms where I loitered
  When spirit and life were young.

But the faces beloved are shadowed,
  Pallid and dim they seem;
And the voices beloved are distant,
  Like voices heard in a dream.

And outstretched hands that beckon,
  Beckon and wave in vain;
The way that my feet have trodden
  They cannot return again.

A pilgrim, I wander onward,
  Weary and travel-worn,
Seeking the low, green gateway
  That leads into endless morn.

WHAT LACK I YET?

WHAT lack I yet? There's sunshine at my door,
    A broad, blue sky above the level moor—
But, oh my life! my life so cold and poor!

What lack I yet? The robins flutter by,
And nests are made; I hear the nestlings cry,
Oh, robin, you are richer far than I.

What lack I yet? Sweet, eager voices call—
The children play beside my garden wall—
I sit, I look and listen—that is all.

What lack I yet? My home, my lands are fair;
I walk, I sleep, I have no pain to bear,
Nor any sting of conscience, weight of care.

What lack I yet ?   My hair is silver gray—
Love was my guest through all the happy day,
But night draws on, and Love hath passed away.

What lack I yet ?   Silence and sleep are best,
God sendeth *peace* unto the weary breast.
What lack I yet, save death's sweet touch, and rest ?

AT SCHOOL.

LAST night I sat by my window,
　　At the dying of the day,
And I heard the soft rain falling
　　From clouds of desolate gray;
Last night I sat by my window,
　　And I thought the drops of rain
Were tears of angels, weeping
　　For life's unending pain.

The wind, in its passionate sobbing,
　　Had sorrowful tales to tell;
And I thought of the time of parting
　　From the friends I have loved so well;
I thought how the forms around me,
　　The faces I see to-day,
Will be gone, and perhaps forever
　　Vanished, like dreams, away!

Again with its wealth of roses,
  Again with its wild flowers sweet,
June will come, but the woodland paths
  Will be trodden by other feet;
And ours will wander whither?—
  Whither, oh, who can tell!
For the coming years are mute as death,
  And guard their secrets well.

But other footsteps lightly
  Will tread the dear old halls,
And other voices will ring out
  Within the dear old walls;
And the bell will sound at eventide,
  To call the loiterers home—
But the feet that now obey it,
  Never again may come:

May be wandering, lost, and weary,
  Out from the shepherd's fold—
To linger no more forever
  In places they knew of old.
And some that I see around me,
  Ere the roses come again—

May be sleeping, long, and deeply,
 The slumber that knows not pain.

But the past will be very sacred,
 With a tender and sad regret,
And its halls will be filled with pictures
 Which the soul cannot forget !
And oft, in the solemn twilight,
 The veil shall seem drawn away,
And once more they will stand around me—
 The friends that I love to-day.

Though my soul may be world-weary,
 My lips may be tired of breath,
And my heart, in its ceaseless beating,
 May long for the calm of death ;
Yet I know that remembrance holy,
 Dear memories' softened glow,
Will give to my weary spirit
 The peace of the long ago.

And the same sky will be o'er me,
 Wherever my feet may be,

And the same strong hand will guide me
  Throughout eternity.
For the paths that on earth may lead us
  From those we love best away,
May come together in heaven,
  In the light of eternal day.

F. E. I.—Spring Term.

HOPELESS.

I SLEEP and wake—I sleep and wake,
  The world it is fair and grand;
The long nights wane and the long days break
  Over a lovely land

Where clover-fields are red as the blush
  On a happy maiden's cheek,
And bluebirds flutter from bush to bush,
  And butterflies hide and seek.

The mountains yearn to the far, blue sky,
  And the silver waters fall,
And dreaming, the happy valleys lie,
  And sunshine is over all!

But, if I could choose between life and death,
  Between the night and the day,
Gladly I'd give unto God my breath,
  Ere an hour had passed away!

HYMN.

LET me not stray,
　　Dear Saviour, lost and weary,
Out from the narrow way,
　The wide is still more dreary;
　　But let one star,
　　　Shining forever o'er me,
　Though faint and far,
　　Be still before me.

Help me to bear
　My faith in Thee unbroken;
Thou hearest prayer
　E'en though unspoken;
　　Grant me above the cross
　　　The crown to see—
　　Heaven nearer by each loss
　　That falls on me!

DREAMLESS.

THEY dream not, slumbering where the sunlight falls,
Where in the summer-time the wild-bird calls
Within the churchyard walls.

They dream not, in unmingled silence blest,
Draining the precious draught of perfect rest;
Pain unto brain or breast.

Comes never—oh, how sweet to lie
All silently beneath the changing sky,
While the long years go by!

EARTH AND HEAVEN.

OH, still October day!
    Long, peaceful, golden hours that glide
Like stately barks on Time's smooth tide,
    To anchor far away.

Oh, kind and loving sky!
The mountains yearn to kiss your face;
Secure and smiling in your grace
    The pleasant valleys lie.

Oh, warm and dreary air—
Blown out of heaven's gate to bless,
Oh, touch me with a soft caress,
    And carry back a prayer.

Oh, Saviour, Lord, and Friend!
How beautiful must heaven be,
Since this fair earth Thou givest me,
    Is beauty without end!
    6

DEATH'S RIVER.

HARK! the pine-trees
   Shake and shiver
By the river;
   Loud the breeze
Blows forever, ever
   In the trees!

Hark! the low sound
Of the dark waves,
While the wind raves
   Cold around,
And the leaves fall, like a death-pall,
   On the ground!

And the bleak night
Bideth ever
By the river;
   But the light
Cometh never, never
   Fair and bright!

FOR SANFORD.

I SAW a picture, Sanford,
  Once in the days gone by—
A glimpse of greenest woodland,
  An arch of summer sky;
A fallen tree all moss-grown,
  In the lonely and silent dell,
And a path that came winding downward,
  Where shine and shadow fell.

And out from the forest dimness,
  Down through that quiet glade,
A boy and girl came loitering,
  In sunshine and in shade;
The light winds played about them,
  The birds sang overhead,
And fallen leaves of last year
  Rustled beneath their tread.

They seemed as a part of spring-time,
   So youthful and glad and fair :
Both had eyes like the deep, deep sea,
   And the girl had golden hair;
And they sat and talked together,
   On the fallen tree in the dell,
While over the shining river
   Came sounds of a distant bell.

Then the youth divided an orange,
   In quarters even and fair,
And she took one and he took one,
   And the other two went—where ?
But it was as pretty a picture
   As ever I have seen,
Lighted with golden sunshine,
   And framed in summer green !

ALBUM OF S. LANDT, F. E. I., 1861.

PATIENCE.

STILL! be still, oh, feverish heart! I long for a
    little rest;
I am so tired of the cross I bear—but whatever God
    wills is best;
Only, the way seems long! I weary of wandering on;
The road grows rougher with every step, and daylight
    is almost gone!

Still! be still, oh, murmuring lips! Close over the
    yearning cry;
The west is dim, but the fair stars shine—safe, safe in
    their happy sky;
And heaven seems nearest when daylight dies, and
    God is forever near—
Still! be still, oh, passionate heart! What is it you
    need to fear?

REMEMBRANCE.

NOW, in the dawn of the spring-time,
　　Just when the first leaves come,
And deep in untrodden woodlands
　　The earliest violets bloom—
How strangely my soul remembers,
　　With pleasure that seems half-pain,
The dear old days that have faded,
　　Never to shine again !

When I look from my open window
　　O'er the marshes brown and bare,
I close my eyes to remember
　　A picture more sweet and fair ;
The fields and the distant mountains,
　　Bathed in the sunset glow,
And dim old woods where our footsteps
　　Went wandering years ago !

I see the glimmering river
  That circled the quiet town,
Spanned by its long, white bridges,
  Where the drift-wood floated down ;
And the elm-trees, tall and stately,
  Shading the village street,
And the lonely walk by the paper-mill,
  Where the lovers used to meet !

And my heart is weary with longing,
  Too weary to hope or pray,
As I loiter beside my window
  This beautiful April day ;
And the sunshine is only sadness,
  And sad is the changing sky ;
But saddest of all, the yearning
  For hours that have long gone by !

AUTUMN PRAYER.

THE crimson and golden garlands,
    Wreaths that the Autumn wore,
Are spreading their soft, soft carpet
    Over earth's barren floor;
And mutely the bare, brown branches
    Stretch up their hands in prayer,
Like souls of the world forgotten,
    Asking God's tender care.

Still are the woodland spaces,
    Still as a room of death;
The stream slides down through the silence,
    Murmuring, under breath;
Like to some patient pilgrim
    In search of the heavenly shore,
Softly she goeth onward,
    Praying forever more.

REQUIESCAT IN PACE.

GOD receive his soul !—Amen.
    Close and seal the wide, dark eyes,
  Where death's awful shadow lies—
Light will never dawn again;
      No more tears to weep,
      No more watch to keep,
      Nothing but endless sleep.

Lay his passive hands at rest,
  In the way that they shall be,
  All throughout eternity.
Cross them idly on his breast;
      Ere yet the work be done,
      Ere yet the web be spun,
      These listless hands begun.

Make his lips meet once for all;
 Never more to smile or pray,
 Or a loving word to say,
Or to answer any call—
  Wan lips so still and cold,
  There is nothing to be told,
  Of the secrets they infold.

Smooth away the soft brown hair
 From the brow where thought lies dead;
 On the heart whence love hath fled
Fold the linen softly down.
  Rest forever, heart and brain;
  Never passion, care, or pain
  Break thine awful peace again !

AFTER FREDERICKSBURG, *December*, 1862.

DAISIES.

THE world is a sea of snow-white daisies,
  I walk knee-deep in the level tide;
Slowly I wade, and the yielding billows
  Part at my coming on either side.

Make me a path through their lowly sweetness;
  See, in my wake, like a track of foam,
Pallid they lie, with their fair heads drooping,
  Sadly marking my pathway home!

Oh, trodden-down daisies! For such brief pleasure,
  To feel your softness under my feet,
Have I made waste of the tender beauty,
  That bees and butterflies find so sweet?

DEGRADED.

WHY did you shrink, with your face half shaded
    And turned from mine, as you floated by?
  You are an innocent woman, and I—
I have fallen, and lie—degraded.

I felt your breath—so near we were crowded,
    And the floating silk of a truant curl;
  I touched your hand, with its ring of pearl—
Your bosom so modestly veiled and shrouded;

Just for a moment—then we parted;
    The crowd gave way, and, with soft, shy grace,
  You turned to look on my sin-worn face,
With some sweet apology—how you started!

As if at the sound of a solemn warning,
    Your warm smile faded—you turned your head;

But why did you shrink from me? I am dead;
And a cold, cold corpse, cannot merit scorning.

Dead as the stones your feet passed over;
  Dead to the passionate dreams of youth;
  Dead to all tenderness, honor, truth,
Dead to the sweetness of love or lover.

Strange, is it not, how a dream can wean us?
  While I stood pressed to you closely there
  Feeling the silk of your soft brown hair,
I had forgotten the gulf between us.

I had crossed over it in my dreaming,
  And that one moment seemed as a light
  Suddenly struck in the heart of night,
Only to die while I blessed its beaming—

Killed by the scorn on your fair young features,
  Killed by their anger and flushing shame;
  Yet we are women—we share the name—
Even, at the least, we are both God's creatures.

Have you forgotten how Christ commanded
  A woman to go and sin no more?
  Do I not carry the stain she bore?
Am I not branded, as she was branded?

Out of His purity He forgave her;
  You must scorn her because she erred!
  You would not drop her a loving word,
Or touch her hand—if a touch could save her!

Oh, Christian charity is the oddest
  Of all the charity under the sun!
  I am a creature to loathe and shun,
But you—you are innocent, pure, and modest.

You are carefully kept and shielded;
  I am sinfully bought and sold;
  Your price is higher than purest gold,
For you have withstood—and I have yielded.

Out of the wonderful wealth God gave you
  Could you not spare me a single mite?
  Child, from a life such as mine, to-night,
I could willingly die to save you.

How should you know that my heart was broken,
   Under my jewels so rich and grand?
   That little ring on your slender hand—
Was it some faithful lover's token?

Do you pray when you first awaken,
   Bend the knee when the day is done?
   God will hear if you plead for one
Of love and mercy and grace forsaken!

One little prayer for a life long shaded,
   Darkened with passion and grief and shame;
   One little prayer in the Saviour's name,
For sake of a woman's soul—degraded!

ANGEL-GUIDE.

" OH, but the path is steep—the burden heavy ! "
    " Courage, beloved—yet a little way ! "
" Oh, but the cold winds blow, and night so dreary
    Hurries to hide the day ! "

" Look how I stumble on the stony pathway—
    Your feet are sure—your wings are strong and light ;
I cannot follow after your swift leading
    When it is darksome night."

" Fear not, beloved—I shall wait thy coming,
    My voice shall warn thee from the precipice ;
Where death and dangers are, my hand shall cover
    And bridge the dark abyss."

" But the day wanes—the last red fires are burning
    Low on the threshold of the happy West ;

And home-lights shine along the warm, green valley
  Where safety is—and rest."

" Look not behind, dear soul—thou canst not tarry ;
  A long and lonely pilgrimage is thine;
But darkness will be pierced with starry splendor,
  And late, the moon will shine."

" Oh, but my heavy cross ! If my strength fail me
  Long ere the mountain-top, what must I do ? "
" If thy strength fail, at last, my arm shall bear thee—
  Thou, and thy burden, too."

7

SO YOUNG.

I WAS so young—so young!
  Gay as the butterfly on its wing—
Over the hedge the roses hung,
  And I heard the oriole sing.
    The merry wind went by,
      Lightly it lifted my floating hair;
    Mine was a blue and cloudless sky,
      And the whole round world was fair!

I was so young—so young!
  I ran through the clover and meadow sweet—
I mocked the birds with my careless tongue
  And the brook with my nimble feet.
    The moths and the dragon-flies,
      I loved to follow them up and down;
    I made of the earth my paradise,
      Its bitterest fruit unknown!

I was so young—so young !
  But is it long since my leafy June ?
Why should my soul seem warped and wrung
  Like an instrument out of tune ?
    I long to grow old and gray—
      It seems that beauty and youth are vain,
    And I would to God I were hidden away
      From my passionate love and pain !

LIGHT LOVE.

YOU loved her well—so well!
   Come, now, and speak your mind.
Have you no pleasant tale to tell,
  No whisper soft and kind?
Passive she lies, and still.
   You loved to murmur in her willing ear—
Now you may cry aloud, or whisper low,
  She will not hear!

Her beauty charmed your soul;
  Draw near and look on her—
Nay, satisfy your ardent gaze!
  She will not flush or stir;
Nor turn aside her head,
  Nor raise her modest eyes.
See, the dark fringe is frozen down,
  No more to rise!

You knew her warm and kind—
  Poor heart, too kind and warm !
Come, now and take her in the old close clasp ;
  She fears not stain or harm.
Nay, but your tears are late !
  You loved her well—so well—
Would you had wept in time to save
  Her soul from hell !

WRITTEN IN SAND.

THE long, white waves ran up the beach,
  And white and silver shone the sand,
As, far beyond the billows' reach,
  I wrote a name upon the strand.

The sea-shells glittered in the sun,
  The snowy fringes softly swept;
Still slowly gaining, one by one,
  Close to my written word they crept.

"Turn, turn, O tide, and spare me yet
  My one dear hope of ended years!"
But while I cried, the waves had wet
  And washed it out with eager tears!

WEARY.

YOU are weary, idle hands; you have no work to
      do;
Diamonds gem your lily fingers like great drops of
      dew—
Fingers slight that twine each other all the long day
      through.

You are weary, sweet red lips ; you have no vow to
      speak—
No impassioned kiss to press against a lover's cheek;
All day long you touch each other, pure and meek.

You are weary, eager eyes, of looking out afar;
In the field there gleams a daisy—in the sky, a star;
Nothing nearer, dearer, than the flower and planet
      are !

www.ingramcontent.com/pod-product-compliance
Lightning Source LLC
Chambersburg PA
CBHW032155010726
47493CB00008BA/2709

* 9 7 8 3 3 3 7 2 6 5 3 3 5 *